An Amazing Story

{ NICE TO READ YOU! }

An Amazing Story
Telma Guimarães

Suplemento de Atividades
Elaborado por Rodrigo Mendonça

NOME: _____
ANO: _____
ESCOLA: _____

Editora do Brasil

Martin has no friends in school, because his classmates think he is weird. But he is very creative, and his teacher decides to help him make friends after reading a great composition he wrote. Everybody gets to know him and his house, but there is something a bit different there...

1. Do you remember these facts from the story? Try to complete the crossword below.

a) Martin's classmates don't know, but his _____ is a ghost.

b) _____ is a celebration when kids get to dress up as ghosts and other characters, and get candies from the adults.

c) Miss _____ is the teacher who decides to help Martin.

d) The other kids said Martin was _____ and weird, but it wasn't true.

e) Witches use a _____ to fly.

f) The ghost _____ wanted to borrow Miss Baldwin's witch costume.

g) _____ is sad, because he doesn't have friends at school.

2. Can you put the sentences below in the correct order? The first one is done as an example.

a) [1] Miss Baldwin reads Martin's story and decides to help him make more friends.

b) [ ] Martin was relieved, his Grandma had fooled everybody pretending to be disguised as a ghost, and he decides to start bringing friends to his house.

c) [ ] All the students got excited and wanted to wear the coolest costumes.

d) [ ] They went to the students' houses to ask for candies.

e) [ ] Elizabeth flies to Miss Baldwin's room to get the dress and scares her. The next day, Miss Baldwin believes it was all a bad dream.

f) [ ] They decided to go inside anyway, and everybody loved Martin's family. Elizabeth asked Miss Baldwin to lend her the dress for a date.

g) [ ] Martin made friends and helped everybody with the preparations.

h) [ ] Martin's house was next but he and Samantha had disappeared.

i) [ ] Martin and Samantha reappeared; they were talking to a neighbor.

j) [ ] Miss Baldwin has an amazing idea after watching TV: she would go trick-or-treating with her students.

b) Teacher Nancy decided to help Martin…
- ☐ …so she decided to make a special Halloween activity.
- ☐ …but she didn't have time.

c) Everybody went to Martin's house…
- ☐ …and they thought his family was very cool.
- ☐ …however, the door was locked and they decided to go to another house.

d) Martin's grandmother was really a ghost…
- ☐ …therefore he decided to move to another house.
- ☐ …but she was also very nice.

8. Based on the previous exercise, match the definitions accordingly.

   a) *But* and *however* are used   ☐ to add ideas.

   b) *And* and *as well* are used   ☐ to draw conclusions.

   d) *So* and *therefore* are used   ☐ to contrast ideas.

9. Christmas, Hannukah, Easter, Carnival etc. are examples of holidays that are traditionally celebrated around the world.

   a) Do you and your family have a tradition? Do you celebrate any holidays with them? Discuss it in groups.

   b) Now, write a paragraph about the tradition you discussed previously. Try to include information on how you celebrate it, when you celebrate it, and who you celebrate it with.

   _____
   _____
   _____
   _____
   _____
   _____
   _____

5. Halloween uses a lot of famous monsters and other famous characters as decoration or costume designs. Do you know their stories? Underline the best alternative to complete the sentences below.

Example:

Vampires usually have (longer/shorter) lives than humans.

   a) Saci Pererê is the (kindest/most mischievous) creature in Brazil.
   b) Werewolves are (weaker/stronger) during the full moon.
   c) Curupira is the (biggest protector/the biggest destroyer) of the forests in Brazil.
   d) Boitatá is the (largest/most adorable) mythical snake in Brazil.
   e) Ogres are much (more beautiful/larger) than humans.
   f) Leprechauns are (bigger/smaller) than humans.

6. Now choose one of the creatures from exercise 5 and research about it. Create a short presentation with the information you discovered, and make sure to include the sentence from exercise 5 as well.

Example:

Vampires usually have longer lives than humans. They are monsters who have the ability to turn into bats, they are very strong and fast, and have very acute senses, but they have to suck on the blood of the living to survive. To kill a vampire, you need to pierce its heart with a wooden stake, but they are also weak against garlic, holly water and crosses.

After that, you will have to present your research to the rest of the class. Use the example above to guide you.

7. How well do you remember the story? Choose the best alternative to complete the sentence.

   a) Martin was a very shy…
      ☐ …but creative boy.
      ☐ …and stubborn boy as well.

3. How much do you know about Halloween? Check if the sentences below are true (T) or false (F). You may need to research to find the answers.

   a) ☐ Halloween is celebrated in November.

   b) ☐ Children disguise as monsters, ghosts or other famous characters, and go from house to house asking for candies.

   c) ☐ Halloween was invented in the United States.

   d) ☐ Halloween is celebrated in Brazil just like it is in the US.

   e) ☐ The children say "trick or treat" and the adults have to give them candies, otherwise the children will play a prank on them.

   f) ☐ Some people like to have Halloween parties with candies, sodas and sometimes even a scary costume contest.

   g) ☐ On Halloween day, children have to find gifts hidden around the house.

4. a) Halloween was recently introduced in Brazil, but it is not so popular yet. Why do you think people in Brazil don't have the habit of celebrating it? Would you like to go trick-or-treating?

   _____
   _____
   _____

   b) What are some Brazilian celebrations you know? How and when are they celebrated? Do you know the story behind their origins?

   _____
   _____
   _____
   _____
   _____

{ NICE TO **READ YOU!** }

An Amazing Story

Telma Guimarães

Ilustrações de Weberson Santiago

Editora do Brasil

© Editora do Brasil S.A., 2014
Todos os direitos reservados
Texto © Telma Guimarães
Ilustrações © Weberson Santiago

DIREÇÃO EXECUTIVA Maria Lúcia Kerr Cavalcante Queiroz
DIREÇÃO EDITORIAL Cibele Mendes Curto Santos
GERÊNCIA EDITORIAL Felipe Ramos Poletti
SUPERVISÃO DE ARTE E EDITORAÇÃO Adelaide Carolina Cerutti
SUPERVISÃO DE CONTROLE DE PROCESSOS EDITORIAIS Marta Dias Portero
SUPERVISÃO DE DIREITOS AUTORAIS Marilisa Bertolone Mendes
SUPERVISÃO DE REVISÃO Dora Helena Feres
EDIÇÃO Gilsandro Vieira Sales
ASSISTÊNCIA EDITORIAL Flora Vaz Manzione
AUXÍLIO EDITORIAL Paulo Fuzinelli
COORDENAÇÃO DE ARTE Maria Aparecida Alves
PRODUÇÃO DE ARTE Obá Editorial
    COORDENAÇÃO Simone Oliveira
    EDIÇÃO Mayara Menezes do Moinho
    PROJETO GRÁFICO E DIAGRAMAÇÃO Thaís Gaal Rupeika
COORDENAÇÃO DE REVISÃO Otacilio Palareti
REVISÃO Equipe EBSA
CONTROLE DE PROCESSOS EDITORIAIS Leila P. Jungstedt e Bruna Alves

DADOS INTERNACIONAIS DE CATALOGAÇÃO NA PUBLICAÇÃO (CIP)
(CÂMARA BRASILEIRA DO LIVRO, SP, BRASIL)

Andrade, Telma Guimarães Castro
   An amazing story/Telma Guimarães;
ilustrações de Weberson Santiago. – 2. ed. –
São Paulo: Editora do Brasil, 2014. – (Nice to read you!)

   ISBN 978-85-10-05471-3

1. Inglês (Ensino fundamental) I. Santiago,
Weberson. II. Título. III. Série.

14-06553   CDD-372.652

ÍNDICES PARA CATÁLOGO SISTEMÁTICO:
1. Inglês : Ensino fundamental   372.652

2ª edição / 1ª impressão, 2014
Impresso na Intergraf Ind. Gráfica Eirelli

Rua Conselheiro Nébias, 887
São Paulo, SP, CEP 01203-001
Fone (11) 3226-0211 – Fax (11) 3222-5583
www.editoradobrasil.com.br

The bell rang a few seconds ago.

"Okay, class. You had enough time to write your compositions."

The students stood up and put their papers on the teacher's desk.

"Bye-bye, have a nice weekend!" said Miss Baldwin, smiling.

"Hurry up, Martin. The class is over."

"Here it is, Miss Baldwin. Hope you like it." The boy gave the teacher his composition.

"I bet I will."

I have fifteen minutes left before my next class. Let me take a look at these compositions. Some of these kids are very creative, especially Martin Dafoe. I think he's so lonely. He doesn't have any friends at all. Well, this is a nice title.

BELIEVE IT OR NOT!

My grandmother is a ghost. Nobody believes me, but it is true. She died many years ago and came back again to live with us.

I was nine when she first appeared. My sister and I were playing in the backyard when we heard a strange noise. We looked around. Nothing.

We went on playing when we heard that noise again. It sounded like chains.

"Martin!" Someone called my name.

We started to run as quickly as we could. I was frightened and so was my sister.

"Martin, Sue, it's grandma. Don't be afraid!" the voice said in a sweet manner.

"Who… who… who are you?" I mumbled.

"I'm grandma Hannah. I'm a ghost now. You can't see me."

"Do you carry chains like a real ghost?" I was scared, but interested.

"Of course I do!" She finally showed herself.

So we became close friends like grandmas and grandsons must be.

Grandma told us that ghosts sometimes wear white sheets to appear. She prefers the pink ones because they are more attractive. She also wears high heels. They are not very common among ghosts, but grandma is not an ordinary ghost.

She hates haunted castles. That's the reason why she chose our house to live in. She told us that it is better to meet other people. "Young ghosts!" She laughed.

We didn't know there were other ghosts there. Can you believe that? There's Camilla, Diana, Charles and Elizabeth. Grandma introduced them to us the other day, during tea time. They are really fun to talk to.

My friends don't like to come over to my house. They say that there are strange noises there. It's a pity because they could meet all those nice ghosts and listen to their funny stories.

My parents don't care if I keep on talking to my ghost friends all day long. They know grandma is also a ghost – they keep her bedroom the way it used to be. They tell me to bring my friends over to our house – but what can I do if they don't like ghost sounds?

I'm very sad, Miss Baldwin. I have no friends. All they say is that I'm nuts and weird, too.

Can you help me? Do I have to send my ghost grandma and her friends away? How can these classmates be friendlier? They call me "Casper", Miss Baldwin. I'm not like "Casper", you know that.

Miss Baldwin was shocked. She couldn't imagine that Martin was such a good writer.

This is what I call an "A" composition, she thought.

The bell rang again and the kids of the seventh grade were about to arrive.

The teacher picked up all the papers and put them away in her briefcase.

One more class and that's over! She was looking forward to that.

As soon as Miss Baldwin finished her class, she went home.

"Nancy, all you need is a nice shower, a fine meal and one of those good movies on TV," she said to herself.

Nancy put on her pajamas, socks, took the popcorn out of the microwave, picked up some vanilla ice-cream, and turned on the TV.

"Popcorn and ice-cream… This is junk food!" she said, laughing.

She switched over the channels until she saw…

"'Amazing Stories'! I like that!" she said.

It was a terrifying story about a woman that had turned into a ghost. She was really fed up with love stories and soap operas.

Nancy saw another movie.

"What a coincidence! It's called 'Phantom' and it's about ghosts, too!"

After that movie, she finally went to bed.

Nancy woke up early. She had slept like a log. After breakfast, she started reading the students' compositions. They were all different from Martin Dafoe's.

Every time I go to the cafeteria I see Martin having lunch by himself. Maybe he is too shy and can't make any friends. But I can try changing this situation! She had an idea.

It was a beautiful Monday morning when Miss Baldwin entered the classroom.

"Your compositions are very nice!" she started. "But you, Martin Dafoe, you gave your best. Congratulations."

Everybody stared at Martin.

The kid was happy. He got an "A".

Some of the students talked to him.

"Great!" Steve Johnson exclaimed.

"That's cool!" Samantha Jones was surprised.

That's a good start! Miss Baldwin was proud of herself.

"Well, I had an idea last night. As you know, Halloween is next Friday and I thought we could 'trick or treat' together," Miss Baldwin told her class. Everybody loved the idea.

"We can even make our costumes with Mrs. Trump, during the Art class. What about that?" she asked the students.

"Great!"

"I'll be Hulk!"

"And I'll be the Beast."

They were so excited that they almost didn't pay any attention to Miss Baldwin's suggestions.

"Calm down, kids. I haven't finished yet. We are going to meet in front of the school and then…"

"What?" they wanted to know.

"We'll go to one another's houses. Isn't that fantastic? The students from Notre

Dame Elementary School trick-or-treating together. Like a team."

The students agreed. All the twenty-five kids were going to scare the inhabitants of Canton City.

They had fun during the week with the sewing and the creation of masks.

Miss Baldwin was happy, too. Martin was feeling perfectly well with the other students. That was all she wanted: friendship, sincerity, work and fun!

"How can I look like a ghost?" Samantha was desperate.

"This is not the right way to put the sheet on!" Martin helped his new friend.

"Thank you, Martin. You have a special manner…"

"Look at these chains! I'm not going to convince anybody this way!" Steve was disappointed.

"Let's try something different." Martin was patient.

"Oh, I like that!" Steve was feeling like the "Phantom of the Opera".

"What are you going to be, Martin?" Ted asked.

"Maybe a ghost. You know, it's easier!"

"Casper, the friendly ghost!" somebody whispered.

Friday finally arrived.

The students were all in their costumes in front of the school. Most of them did look like monsters and ghosts.

Miss Baldwin was dressed up like a witch. She looked awful.

"Oh, Miss Baldwin, you are so…"

"Disgusting!" She laughed at her own fancy dress and her funny make-up. "Are you ready, class?" she cried.

"Yes!"

"Trick or treat! Here we go to Mike's house first!" she decided.

It was funny.

Mike's mother opened the front door and screamed.

After the first impact, she recognized some of the children and gave them sweets.

Then there came Susan's house, Bill's, Ted's, Mary Ann's, Steve's, George's, Martha's, and Samantha's.

Samantha's mother couldn't understand how Miss Baldwin could look so ugly and disgusting.

"Well, congratulations on your make-up. It's perfect! You really look like a witch," Mrs. Jones praised.

"Martin's house now, kids!" Miss Baldwin pointed at the boy's two-storey house.

Everybody followed her.

Well, my plan is working out. They are better friends now. She smiled.

They rang the bell. The door was open.

"Martin, where are you?" Miss Baldwin looked around.

"I can't see Martin and Samantha. Where are they?" Ted asked.

"I'm going to call them. I'll be right back!" Mary Ann said.

"Let's get into the house."

"Trick or treat!" they shouted.

"Come in. We are in the kitchen!" They heard a woman's voice. "Oh, what a lovely group!"

Miss Baldwin and her students came to the kitchen door. There were three people dressed like ghosts, sitting around the table.

"Oh, it's Halloween! How do you like our costumes, dear? We always try to get into the spirit of the party!" the one in a pink sheet spoke first.

"How funny!" everybody cried.

"Hey, your clothes are fantastic!" Steve was impressed.

"Are you Martin's parents?" Martha wanted to know.

"Are you Martin's schoolmates?" a man's voice wanted to know.

"Yes!" they said. "Trick or treat!" they asked the three ghosts in the kitchen.

"These are for you, kids: Ghost Chocolates, Phantom Candies, Witch Cookies," the ghost woman offered.

"Thanks, Mrs. Dafoe," Steve said.

"Thanks, Mr. Dafoe!" Martha exclaimed.

"That's cool, Sue!" Ted was deeply impressed. Martin's sister really looked like a ghost!

The kids were discussing:

"Our families could do the same next Halloween."

"Martin's parents were much more creative. And joined the spirit of the party!"

"Martin Dafoe is a nice guy!"

The ghost teenager looked at the witch's clothes and said: "Oh, I love your clothes, sweetheart!"

"Isn't she sweet? She's trying to be nice!" Miss Baldwin laughed.

"Maybe you can lend it to me. I have a date tomorrow night!" the girl added.

"Of course!" Miss Baldwin agreed. "You can come over to my house at midnight. It will be a pleasure."

"Bye-bye!" They left Martin's house.

"Come back soon, fellows!" The ghosts said goodbye.

"Isn't that great? Look at these sweets. They are the best!" The students were happy. "We didn't see strange things at Martin's house. People used to say he is nuts. That's a big lie! Everything there is…"

"Absolutely normal!" Miss Baldwin completed. "Let's go to Ted's house now."

Nancy Baldwin was very proud of herself. A few moments ago they were at Martin's house. His family was perfect and the students loved them. She specially liked the one who asked for her dress. Martin and his family had a great sense of humor.

Maybe he is going to be a writer someday. He is probably going to write television programs like "Amazing Stories". Or one day he can also be a "ghost-writer"... She smiled at her own joke.

"Look! There come Martin and Samantha. Hey, where were you? We were looking for you," Steve cried.

Martin explained that some people thought that he and Samantha were real ghosts. Miss Emma and her sister were in their eighties and could hardly see. They didn't know it was Halloween and when they saw those two people dressed like ghosts in their backyard, they started screaming.

"Haven't you heard their cries?" Samantha looked serious.

"No, Samantha. We were at Martin's house". Miss Baldwin explained.

"Oh, that would be a lovely scene to watch: Miss Emma and Miss Aretha having those attacks!" Steve said.

Martin was pale.

"You were… at my house?"

"In your kitchen, to be more exact," Steve spoke first.

"Your family is cool!" Mary Ann joined the rest of the group.

"Great!" George showed the sweets. "A lot of candies with funny names!"

"Fabulous!" Ted added.

"Fantastic!" Bill was jealous.

Martin is a lucky kid! The other families are not so creative. For nothing in the world they would dress like ghosts, thought Miss Baldwin.

Martin is not like "Casper". That is just a silly joke! Mike thought. He promised himself not to call him that way again.

Martin didn't know what to say. Everything seemed to be under control. Everybody wanted to go on knocking at the schoolmates' houses asking for more candies.

It was almost midnight when they decided to go home.

Martin was excited. Everybody loved his family — although he didn't tell his friends that his family had left the city the night before.

"How did you fool them?" he asked grandma as soon as he got home.

"Well, we were having dinner at that moment," she explained.

"We… who?" Martin became white again.

"Charles, Elizabeth and I, of course. Elizabeth looked just like your sister with her blonde hair."

"Grandma!" Martin was astonished.

"We tried to look natural, that was all. We didn't even scream when we saw that awful witch. I approved of your friends, Martin. I can't understand why you don't invite them to come over here!" Grandma shook her head and went on. "But don't trust witches. They are not reliable!"

"Oh, don't worry about the witch, grandma. She's harmless. And from now on I promise that my friends will visit me."

Martin kissed grandma and his friends Charles and Elizabeth before going to bed. He was very tired, but extremely happy.

"I think you're right, grandma. Martin must be careful about his friends. There's a lot of weird people around!" Charles agreed.

"Except the witch!" Elizabeth sighed. "She seemed so sincere in that lovely, lovely dress!"

Nancy Baldwin was feeling great.

She went upstairs and entered her bedroom. She looked at herself in the mirror.

"Nice work, Nancy. You should be a psychologist, not a teacher. Now it's time to remove the wig, the purple nails, the make-up, the false nose, the wart." Nancy was talking to herself.

"May I come in?" someone asked.

"What's going on? There's a voice coming from… the window!" Nancy opened the curtains.

"May I come in, dear? It's me, Elizabeth!"

Nancy was surprised.

She opened the window and stared at the guest.

"It's about the dress. You said that around midnight I could come over and borrow your dress," Elizabeth tried to explain.

"How did you climb up here? Did you use a ladder?" Nancy recognized Martin's sister in a sheet.

"There is no ladder, honey. Ghosts don't need them. See, I can fly! The only difference between us is that you need a broom and I don't…"

Elizabeth was beginning to explain that her clothes were not a costume, but Nancy fainted before she could say something.

When she woke up, she imagined, "it was all a bad dream."

I think that I have been watching too many amazing stories on TV lately, she thought.

Glossary}

In alphabetical order

although	embora; apesar de		
amazing	assombroso; surpreendente		
		disgusting	repulsivo, desagradável
as soon as	assim que		
at all	absolutamente; de jeito nenhum	**fancy dress**	fantasia (roupa)
		friendship	amizade
briefcase	pasta	**from now on**	de agora em diante
broom	vassoura	**ghost-writer**	escritor profissional que escreve livros assinados por outros; trocadilho com a palavra "ghost" – fantasma
Casper	Gasparzinho (personagem de história em quadrinhos)		
chain	corrente		
close friends	amigos íntimos	**hardly**	mal; com dificuldade
costume	fantasia (roupa)		
date	encontro	**harmless**	inofensivo
deeply	profundamente; bastante	**haunted castle**	castelo mal--assombrado

ordinary	comum
own	próprio
pale	pálido
pity	pena
pleasure	prazer
reliable	confiável
sewing	costura
sheet	lençol
silly	bobo; tolo
soap opera	novela de TV
sweetheart	querida; doçura
to add	acrescentar
to ask for	pedir
to be about to arrive	estar prestes a chegar
to be astonished	estar surpreso
to be careful	ter cuidado
to be fed up with	estar farto de; não aguentar mais

high heels	sapatos de salto alto
honey	querida; benzinho
joke	piada
junk food	comida pouco saudável ou nutritiva
just	exatamente
ladder	escada
lately	ultimamente
manner	jeito; modo
most	a maioria
nail	unha
(not) even	(nem) mesmo
nuts	maluco

to be frightened	ficar com medo; estar amedrontado	to knock (at)	bater
		to lend	emprestar
to be in the eighties	estar na casa dos oitenta anos	to look for	procurar
		to look forward to	aguardar ansiosamente
to be jealous	ficar com ciúmes; ter inveja	to look like	parecer; assemelhar-se
to be over	estar terminado; acabar		
		to mumble	murmurar
to be proud (of)	estar orgulhoso (de)	to praise	elogiar
to be scared	ficar assustado ou amedrontado	to recognize	reconhecer
		to scare	assustar
to bet	apostar	to scream	gritar
to borrow	tomar emprestado	to seem	parecer
to care	importar-se	to shake	balançar
to climb	subir	to shout	gritar
to faint	desmaiar		
to fool	enganar		
to go on	continuar		
to hurry up	apressar-se		
to invite	convidar		
to join	acompanhar; juntar-se a		
to keep on	continuar		
to keep	conservar; manter		

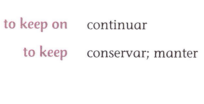

to try	tentar; experimentar
to turn into	transformar-se
to whisper	sussurrar
to work out	funcionar
trick or treat:	"gostosuras ou travessuras", expressão usada pelas crianças que vão de casa em casa pedindo balas e doces
two-storey house	sobrado; casa de dois andares
to sigh	suspirar
to sleep like a log	dormir profundamente; dormir como uma pedra
to sound like	soar como; ter som semelhante a
to stare (at)	encarar; olhar fixamente
to switch over the channels	mudar de um canal para outro
to trust	confiar
used (to)	costumava
wart	verruga
way	modo; jeito
weird	esquisito
What about that?	Que tal?
What's going on?	O que está havendo?
wig	peruca
witch	bruxa
yet	ainda

About the author...

Telma Guimarães is a Brazilian writer of books for children and young people. She graduated in Portuguese and English, which explains why she loves writing in these languages. She loves literature and books, and she has already published a lot of good, fun, and creative stories. Telma lives in Campinas, a city in the state of São Paulo, Brazil. She is married and a mother of three kids. She also has a granddaughter, with whom she shares a lot of stories.

About the illustrator...

Weberson Santiago was born in São Bernardo do Campo, in 1983. He was raised in Mauá and lived for some time in São Paulo, but nowadays he lives in Mogi das Cruzes. Besides illustrating books, Weberson also writes. He teaches at the University of Mogi das Cruzes and at Quanta Academia de Artes.

Este livro foi composto com a família tipográfica
Stone Informal, para a Editora do Brasil, em maio de 2014.